Puff
and the Incredible
Mr. Nobody

by Romeo Muller

Illustrations by Fred Wolf and Chuck Swenson
Based on the TV special

TROLL ASSOCIATES

Puff and the Incredible Mr. Nobody
is an original publication of Troll Books.
This work has never before appeared in book form.

"Never Was a Feather"
Words and Music by Peter Yarrow
Copyright © 1982 by Silver Dawn Music

"Imaginary Friends"
Words and Music by Peter Yarrow
Copyright © 1982 by Silver Dawn Music

Illustrations by Fred Wolf and Chuck Swenson
based on the TV special.

Troll Books
A division of Troll Associates
320 Route 17
Mahwah, New Jersey 07430

Copyright © 1982 by The My Company.
Published by arrangement with The My Company.
Library of Congress Catalog Card Number: 82-51-114.
ISBN: 0-89375-869-8

First Troll Printing, January 1984.

Printed in the United States of America

This book is dedicated to
Kerry Bloor

CONTENTS

SONGS

CHAPTER ONE

The None
and Only

Once, not too long ago, there was Nobody.

If Nobody was in a room by himself, the room was deserted.

When Nobody rode up, he always jumped off an empty bike.

If Nobody had lunch with a friend, the friend ate alone.

Who cares about Nobody, you ask? *Somebody* did. He was a little boy named Terry.

And to him, Nobody was as real as a brother or best friend.

Terry was a very special person, gifted with a hidden wonder that others just did not perceive. Even when he was three years old, he mystified his family and friends. For instance, there was a large zigzag crack in the stucco of the back wall of Terry's house. To everyone else it was simply an ordinary zigzag crack in the stucco.

But when little Terry looked at it, it became, in his mind, an enchanted pathway zigging and zagging magically as it climbed toward that golden place where the sun lives.

By the time he was four, Terry's very special qualities confused those around him and made them jealous. He was quite lonely and needed a very special kind of friend. And so, one night, he selected the brightest star outside his bedroom window and wished for a companion of his own frame of mind to share wonders and discoveries, joys and disappointments, trinkets and treasures.

But there was nobody to fill that need. And, since nobody was all Terry had, he wished for a friend named Nobody.

"Let him come from the sky in my dresser

drawer. And let him look like that duck I always make up, with a saucepan hat and a feather! You know, a regular Nobody."

"You called?" The voice sounded from across the room.

Terry saw that the second drawer of his dresser had popped open. A wonderfully happy-looking duck sat there, fully dressed, brushing star fuzz from his sleeves, wearing a feathered saucepan for a hat.

"I've been waiting so long for you, Nobody!" cried Terry. "Want to do something together?"

Nobody climbed out of the drawer, leaped to the floor, and waddled briskly over to Terry's bed. "If I had a middle name, *Together* would be it!" he joked.

The none-and-only Mr. Nobody had finally danced his way into Terry's life. He climbed up onto the bed, and the two of them started bouncing about, giggling wonderfully, pretending to be corn popping in a perking pot.

"So what's new?" asked Nobody when they had finally stopped bouncing. "Find out anything today?"

"Un-huh," said Terry, nodding yes. "Flowers sing!"

"Really?" said Nobody. He leaned over and listened with amazement to the flowers in the small vase on the bedside table. "By golly, you're right! And the song is 'Frère Jacques'!"

Was this not a wonderful duck? Terry had tried all day to identify the melody.

"Got any new squishy jokes?" Nobody asked casually.

Terry could hardly believe his ears. He thought he was the only person in the whole universe who knew what squishy jokes were, and who appreciated them. "You like squishy jokes too?" he cried.

"If I had a middle name, *Squishy* would be it," said Nobody emphatically.

"Well, I'm working on this new one," said Terry. "But I've only got the first two lines. Maybe you can help with the rest." He started to recite:

"Never was a feather
And no one knew the rules."

"I know!" volunteered Nobody. He recited:

"And that's how all the cherries went . . ."

11

And they both thought of the last line together:

"To squish in squishy pools!"

"WOW! WE WRITE GREAT SQUISHY STUFF TOGETHER!" cheered Terry.

Terry's wish for a special friend had finally come true. They laughed and played together for more than a year. Then, eventually, came that day all kids get to know sooner or later. The first day of school had arrived.

His mom and dad drove Terry in the car that bright September morning. They sat together in the front, and Terry sat in the back with Nobody, who was, of course, invisible to the grownups.

"You're not nervous, are you, Terry?" asked his mother.

Terry's dad glimpsed him in the rearview mirror. Terry gulped, obviously *very* nervous. But he said bravely, "Not me. It's Nobody's first day too. Nobody's not nervous. So I'm not either."

His mom and dad exchanged a worried glance. "Imaginary friends are okay at his age, dear," said Terry's dad. "He'll outgrow Nobody—I hope."

Terry grew, all right, like Jack's beanstalk. He outgrew his shirt and his trousers and his shoes, but he didn't outgrow his special friend, Nobody.

As the months passed they did everything together: homework, cleaning up their room, drawing pictures, looking through the microscope at squiggles, practicing the piano, lying on their backs and sculpting clouds into great scenes.

And if Terry's body grew fast, his mind grew even faster. Like a rocket. Maybe that was because his invisible friend, Mr. Nobody, was always with him. It was like having a soul mate in his pocket.

CHAPTER TWO

How to Lose a Duck and Gain a Dragon

"I love pasghetti!"

Terry and Nobody sat by the large kitchen window, eating their lunch and watching the early February snow fall outside.

Bright as he was, Terry, like most kids, pronounced spaghetti *pasghetti*.

Nobody slurped about thirteen feet of it up in one long string, sighed happily, then wiped his bill with his napkin. "If I had a middle name, *Pasghetti* would be it."

"You know what else I love?" asked Terry. "Weather! I wish I could eat it! Like pasghetti!"

Nobody was delighted with the sudden turn Terry's mind had taken. "Slurp down a rainstorm?" he giggled.

Terry nodded, then got another great idea. "What if, instead of raining or snowing, it pasghettied! You know? All red and slippery, it squiggles down from the sky and makes noodle houses, macaroni trees and flowers and hills—"

"I know what you mean," said Nobody. "But I don't think anybody else will unless we paint a picture."

"Great idea!" cried Terry. They got out the paint jars and covered a large sheet of drawing paper with wonderfully fanciful tomato-colored landscapes.

Unfortunately, the next day at school Terry's art teacher did not think the idea was so great. "Terry, this picture is just silly. You must paint real trees and houses, not spaghetti."

Terry looked away miserably and muttered, "It's pasghetti."

"Real trees. Real houses," continued the art teacher. "And make *sure* nobody helps you."

"I'll make sure, all right. I'll make *real* sure," said Terry under his breath. "From here on I'll just tell them Nobody did it. Then I won't get blamed."

And so Terry began to hide all his talents behind Nobody. Any time he had a thought which was bright, meaningful or offbeat, he'd pretend it came from his best friend.

And pretty soon Terry began to believe what he had started out to pretend. He really thought all his talents originated with Mr. Nobody.

Then came that awful day with the

terrible-tempered Professor Katzendorfer. You see, Terry's school principal was so impressed with his piano playing that he recommended Terry to old Katzendorfer, one of the world's most famous music teachers.

The imposing busts of Beethoven, Mozart and Bach looked down from the mantle on the musty music studio, as the angry-spirited old Professor sputtered at Terry, who sat cringing at the piano.

The whole lesson had started off wrong. To audition, Terry had played an original composition. Impressed, Katzendorfer asked who wrote it. Terry, of course, answered, "Nobody."

The Professor, of course, became totally confused. Then, when Terry explained that Nobody was a duck, and invisible, old Katzendorfer became furious. He thought Terry was trying to make a fool of him. Terry's mom and dad tried to explain, but he would have none of it. The angry Professor threw up his hands and dismissed them curtly.

"Take him home and don't bring him back till he wishes to be serious!"

Driving back in the car, Terry's mom and dad realized something had to be done. And so, that night at the dinner table, Terry's dad had a heart-to-heart talk with his son.

"Son, you know we love you very much," he said.

"I know that, Dad," said Terry. He gestured toward the empty chair next to him. "Both of us do."

Terry's dad gulped and began. He attempted to explain to his son that Nobody was just an imaginary friend. He spoke with infinite kindness, picking and choosing his words with care. But the more he spoke, the more confused Terry became.

Suddenly Terry looked to the chair next to him. It was empty. Nobody was gone! He looked back to his mom and dad and cried out, "What did you do to him? You made him run away!"

He ran upstairs, his small chest heaving with sobs, and threw himself on his bed. And that night, for the first time in more than a year, Terry was alone in his room.

Imaginary friend or not, Terry was nobody without Nobody. He lost interest. His marks dropped off in school. Who would laugh at his squishy jokes now?

And then one night after his mother had tucked him into bed and closed the door, Terry got up, took the sheets off his bed, tied them into a long rope, and dropped one end out of the window. He tied the other end to the bed, then slowly dressed himself, and finally climbed out.

Terry, determined to find his friend, was running away. But since his friend wasn't there to help him tie the sheets correctly, the knots became undone, and Terry began to fall.

"OWWWWWWW!" he cried out as he tumbled down.

PLOP! He landed in two soft things. At the end of one there was a left paw, and at the end of the other, a right paw. They were arms. Dragon arms. And, wonder of wonders, they were attached to a complete dragon. Not only was he complete—he was magic.

Terry didn't realize it yet, but he had the good fortune to be caught by Puff the Magic Dragon!

CHAPTER THREE

A Journey into the Fantaverse

 **P**uff looked playfully toward the skies. "Dear me, is it raining children? Or are you from outer space? Did you slip from a satellite?"

"N-no sir," answered Terry, a bit frightened. "I come from that house."

Puff frowned. "That house? Impossible. *Nobody* lives there!"

Terry's eyes lit up. "You know him too?"

Puff nodded yes. "A distant cousin, but a close companion. He lives there with a chap named Terry."

"*I'm* Terry!"

Puff studied the boy. "By golly, you're right! He's told me all about you. Did he— ahem—ever mention me? Puff? Puff the Magic Dragon?"

Terry gaped at the scaly old fellow. It was the first time he was ever in the presence of a genuine celebrity. "Why, he taught me a song about you. We played it on the piano!" exclaimed Terry. Then he became sad. "But Nobody's gone now. He ran away. I'm going to look for him."

Puff's face brightened. "A search for Nobody? How intriguing. May I join you?"

Terry put out his hand. "Any friend of Nobody is a friend of mine."

They shook hands heartily. But at the end of the shake, Terry did not let go. Instead he started to lead Puff along. "Now come on!" he shouted.

"Which way?" asked Puff.

Terry's face fell. "I don't know. I didn't think about that." He became quite glum. "Aw gee, Nobody always helped me make plans."

Puff thought, then said, "Well, we can go to the right or to the left, or—we can take *that* road!" He pointed to the stucco crack in the rear wall of the house.

Terry looked. It had been a long time since he noticed it. Suddenly Puff blew a magic smoke ring. It drifted over and encircled the

wall crack. In an instant the crack became the magical road through the clouds. The selfsame road Terry had imagined as a small child. The road to where the sun lived!

Forgetting all the rules of time, space and matter, Terry and Puff leaped through the smoke ring and landed on that road. They began to run toward the horizon.

"I bet Nobody's just around that bend! Come on!" cried Terry.

The road zigged magically and zagged wonderfully for miles and miles through the golden clouds. Eventually Puff and Terry came to a sign which said:

WELCOME TO THE FANTAVERSE

"What's the Fantaverse?" asked Terry.

Puff explained, "As the Universe is to real people, so the Fantaverse is to imaginaries."

It sounded like the perfect place for Nobody. Terry rushed forward. But just around the bend he found his way barred by a red and white gate blocking the road.

The Gatekeeper, a fat, funny little fellow wearing an elaborate uniform, waddled out of his hut and moved over to them. "You can't cross the border unless you fill out the proper forms," he said, waving some papers about.

Terry gasped, for he noticed the Gatekeeper was wearing Nobody's saucepan hat.

"Nobody forgot it when he passed through," explained the Gatekeeper.

"He *is* here! But where?"

"Oh way off," said the Gatekeeper, "in the Duckpond of Delights. But *you* can't go there until you fill out these forms." He handed an official-looking document to Terry.

Terry studied it impatiently. "This is blank," he said.

"Not blank," said the Gatekeeper, "Merely expectant. It expects you to write a poem on it."

"A poem?" said Puff. "Write one of those *squishy* ones." He made a pencil appear out of thin air and handed it to Terry.

The boy pulled back. "But I can't. Not without Nobody to help me. It's different when Nobody helps. See, he's always there when all the kids make fun of me and call me names and—"

Puff frowned and nodded to the right. "*Those* kind of kids?" he asked.

Suddenly three kids popped out of

26

Terry's memory and stood in front of him. It wasn't a pleasant memory. There were two boys and a girl, all slightly larger than Terry. They made faces and mocked his poetry.

"Terry is an egghead."

"Anybody who writes poems is a jerk!"

"Get out of here, creep!"

Terry cringed. "Make them go away, Puff!" he begged.

"I'll do better," smiled Puff. "I'll make them come closer. I'll show you what they are *really* saying." He blew a smoke ring. It drifted in front of the kids. Puff brought Terry over and indicated that he should look through the ring.

"See how they are through one of my magic smoke rings."

The kids looked at Terry longingly. "Boy, I'd give anything to make words the way he does," one said.

Another nodded and said, "I'd make up lines for songs that would help turn bad things into good."

The third kid sighed. "I'd just write something pretty for Mom on her birthday."

Suddenly the smoke ring faded. The kids all seemed nasty again.

27

Puff turned to Terry. "Envy, Terry. That's all it is. That confused, unfulfilled longing, bubbling and festering deep inside, confounding the heart, and turning kind tongues cruel. You should feel sorry for them, not afraid."

"I guess so," said Terry.

Puff pointed to the poem-less blank piece of paper. "Go ahead. Time's awasting."

Terry nodded yes and, completely forgetting about the envious kids, began to scribble. When he was finished, he brought it to the Gatekeeper, who adjusted his glasses and began to read:

> *"The night is more night*
> *The gray is more gray,*
> *And empty's more empty*
> *When friends go away.*
>
> *The sun's on the flowers*
> *The rain's full of song,*
> *When friends get together*
> *Where true friends belong."*

"Is it okay?" asked Terry. "Can I get past the gate?"

The Gatekeeper brushed away a tear, removed the saucepan hat from his head and

placed it on Terry's. "Here! I wish it were a wreath of laurel!" The poem was obviously a good deal more than *okay*.

He handed Terry a map and explained, "This will help you find the Duckpond of Delights and Mr. Nobody." Then he became very official and, pulling a rope which raised the gate, announced, "YOU MAY ENTER THE FANTAVERSE!"

CHAPTER FOUR

The Beast Beyond Pasghettiland

 **O**nce they were past the gate Puff said, "I knew you could write a poem by yourself."

Terry shook his head sadly. "Nah. I was *thinking* of Nobody. Besides, I think your pencil is magic."

Puff sighed. How would he ever convince this child?

A few miles farther, they came to a fork in the road. They had to consult the map.

"The Duckpond of Delights is straight ahead," said Terry, reading from the map. " *'Proceed through landscape,'* it says. What landscape?"

"The one right in front of you," answered Puff.

Terry looked up to find that a huge picture frame had appeared suddenly. It framed a spectacular rendering of Terry's old Pasghetti-land painting.

"Wow, Puff! That's so real-looking I bet we could walk right into it!"

"Why not? This *is* the Fantaverse! Come along." He took Terry by the hand and led him into the picture. "Ah," said Puff. "A Nation of Noodles. A Principality of Pasta. A Metropolis of Macaroni!"

Suddenly Puff stopped and pointed toward a raging, steaming red river which lay ahead of them, directly in their path. Terry tried to find it on the map.

"Here it is, Puff. The Marinara River!"

"I had a feeling it wasn't the Mississippi."

"The directions say, *'Draw a boat to get across.'*"

"Cle-*ver*!" said Puff, looking about. "Aha! There are pencils and paints over there." He led Terry to a large pile of art supplies near the river bank.

Terry pulled back, unsure again. "I...I ...can't draw anymore. Not without Nobody."

"Then I suppose it's up to me," sighed Puff, grabbing a paintbrush. He swirled it about and painted a huge banana in midair. Being a magic dragon, he didn't need a canvas or piece of paper to make a picture.

"We can't cross a river on a banana," moaned Terry.

"I'll try again," chuckled Puff, waving the brush about and creating a rocking chair!

"A rocking chair's no good, Puff. A boat! We need a boat!"

Puff swirled the paintbrush once more and ended up with a perfect copy of *Whistler's Mother*. He stepped back to admire his work. "Definitely not seaworthy," said Puff, shrugging helplessly. He wiped his artwork away. "It's up to you, Terry. A pasghetti boat to cross the Marinara River!"

Terry shuddered. "But I can't paint silly stuff like that. My teacher said it was dumb and not real."

"You mean she didn't share your vision, child?"

Terry was puzzled. "What are you talking about?" he asked.

"Your teacher's world was the drab, old ordinary world most of us know. Here, let me show you." He took a deep breath and blew a smoke ring. And like all of Puff's magic smoke rings, this showed things as they really were. He and Terry looked through the ring and saw what appeared to be the world! But this world had a face that looked quite gloomy. A stuffy little felt hat was plopped on top, completely covering the North Pole. And little arms and legs poked out from below.

Puff, of course, seemed to be on familiar terms. "What's new, Mr. World?"

The world could only groan wearily.

Terry couldn't believe what he was seeing. "Is that what the world's really like?" he asked.

"Unless someone like you comes along," answered Puff. He reached into his pocket and produced a pair of colored glasses which

glittered magically. "Here, look at the world through Terry-colored glasses." He popped the glasses onto Terry, who looked at Mr. World again.

A remarkable change had taken place. The happy old world was bursting with every color of the rainbow. He danced about giddily, and for a hat, he wore a *feathered saucepan*!

"I really make Mr. World like that?" asked Terry, unbelieving.

"You, and a precious handful *like* you," answered Puff. "Be you a dozen or a million, you give the gift of a vision unique!" He took the glasses from Terry and glanced through them himself. "Better than Broadway!" he grinned happily, then caused them to disappear in a puff of golden smoke.

"Terry," he continued, "you can reach up and place a star in the sky. So don't worry what people say—people who can't even screw in a light bulb."

A little bit awed, and terribly encouraged for the moment, Terry grabbed the paintbrush and swirled it about. A nifty little sailboat appeared, with a rigatoni hull and a large lasagna noodle for a sail!

"YOU DID IT!" roared Puff. "The S.S. Pasghetti, if ever I saw it!"

A little later, as they were sailing across the river, Terry had second thoughts. "Maybe it wasn't me," he muttered. "Maybe I could paint this boat only because I was wearing Nobody's hat."

Puff sighed. *What will it take to convince this child?* he wondered. He suddenly got an

idea. He puckered up and blew with all his might. The wind he raised caused the saucepan hat to fly off Terry's head.

"PUFF! THE WIND BLEW NOBODY'S HAT AWAY!"

"Guess you're on your own now," said Puff casually.

About halfway across, the river changed from red to blue, and all sights and smells of pasghetti seemed to vanish. Instead, Terry could hear the far-off tinkling of piano keys.

Once ashore, Puff and Terry found they had landed in Cleftomania, the Kingdom of Music. Terry consulted his map. They were getting nearer and nearer to the fabulous Duckpond of Delights.

Cleftomania was perhaps the most fantastic-looking place in the entire Fantaverse. The main road was like a huge piano keyboard stretching to the horizon. Music notes hung from trees, and the trees themselves resembled giant music clefs. Musical instruments seemed to be growing all over. There were violins, horns, drums, trumpets, harps and trombones.

"The map says to *'proceed harmoniously through,'*" said Terry, as he and Puff walked into the long shadows cast by three giant stone heads.

They were the same as the busts in the music teacher's studio, likenesses of Mozart, Beethoven and Bach. At the sound of Terry's voice, they seemed to come to life.

"Harmony, hah!" rumbled Beethoven. "Zere ist no more harmony."

"Ach, Ludwig, you give up too easily," purred the bust of Mozart. "Am I correct, Johann Sebastian?"

The bust of Bach frowned and shook its head glumly. "Nein, Wolfgang," it said to Mozart. "It is *you* who are too optimistic."

"What is going on around here?" asked Puff, looking up at the huge heads.

"A terrible savage beast holds all of Cleftomania in its power," answered Beethoven.

"We are helpless," sighed Bach.

"I've heard that music has charms to soothe the savage beast," said Puff. "Surely you fellows can make music."

Mozart snorted. "And how can we play music? We've got no hands."

"We're such *busts*!" said Bach.

Suddenly there was a terrible, terrible noise, as if every musical instrument in the entire world were in one huge orchestra, and the whole orchestra was playing a sour note.

"IT'S THE SAVAGE BEAST!!" cried all three busts at once.

CHAPTER FIVE

The Duckpond of Delights

Terry looked and saw a truly terrible creature. It was like an ape with fangs and blazing eyes. Over its shoulder it carried a great club. And its ugly mouth was wide open, emitting the discordant sound.

Puff and Terry huddled together. "What can we do, Puff?" cried Terry.

"I guess it's up to you to soothe him," said Puff, reaching up and plucking down a flute

which was growing on a flute tree. He handed it to Terry. "Play one of those tunes you composed."

Terry moaned. "But I *didn't* compose them. *Nobody* did. Don't you understand?" he cried, clutching Puff. "That music didn't come from *me*!"

"Nonsense," said Puff sharply. "It came from everywhere—through *you*!"

Terry was startled by Puff's tone. Then the magic dragon smiled. "Here, let me show you how it works." He blew a magic smoke ring, and both of them looked through it.

Terry saw some birds in a blossom-covered tree. Their twittering suddenly became the sound of flutes and piccolos. Then there were children playing in the cool grass below. Their laughing sounds were suddenly like trumpets and horns. A bumblebee flew by and joined some others. Their sounds were suddenly the drones of a slide trombone. A funny-looking man came along and started to swat the bees with a rolled up newspaper. He missed the bees but hit everything else in sight. And the sounds of his hits became like the rat-a-tat-tat of drumbeats.

Everything was music to Terry.

And then he saw a young mother with her sleeping baby in her arms. She hummed a lullaby, and it became the sound of gentle violins and cellos.

Now all the different instrument sounds came together as one, and it sounded like a beautiful orchestra playing a magnificent melody which was being heard for the very first time. And the very first heart to hear that melody was Terry's. He realized that nobody else would ever hear this music that was unique to him, unless he somehow was able to share it.

And that's just what he did. He raised the flute to his lips and played the melody in his heart.

When they heard the music, the old busts smiled and thought of the happy times so many years ago when they, like Terry, let the world first hear their private sounds. They nodded in time, then looked in wonder at the savage beast.

He was dancing! And wonder of wonders, the music had transformed him into a huge, cuddly kitten.

"I knew there was something to that old saying," chuckled Puff.

Later, as Puff and Terry continued along the road, having passed out of Cleftomania, Terry still couldn't believe the wonder of it all.

"The music was *mine*, Puff!" he cried. "It came from me. Can you *believe* it?"

Puff smiled wryly. "I'll work on it," he said. "But what's this? Can you read that sign up ahead?" His eyes brightened, and he pointed.

The words were quite easy to make out, and they caused Terry's heart to skip a beat:

THE DUCKPOND OF DELIGHTS

There, in front of them, was suddenly a lovely lake, surrounded by blossoming bushes. Many ducks were splashing in the water. And *each one of them looked exactly like Nobody*, saucepan hats and all!

Terry, a bit confused, rushed to the bank, shouting, "HEY, NOBODY! IT'S ME!"

Then a strange thing happened. All of the ducks turned around and spoke at the same time. "HI, TERRY. IT'S ME TOO!"

Terry stopped short and scratched his head. "Hey, which one of you guys is Nobody?"

"I AM!" they all answered.

Terry turned to Puff. "They can't all be Nobody," he said.

"But they all look alike," said Puff. "How will we ever find out which one is real?"

Terry suddenly got a wonderful idea. "Puff! Blow a smoke ring so I can see what they're really like. Then I'll know which one is Nobody!"

Puff grinned. "Oh, why didn't I think of that?" he said playfully. He took a deep, deep breath and then blew a beauty—big enough to circle the entire duckpond.

Terry looked through the ring. The pond still seemed to be full of ducks. Ducks all over the place! No! Wait a minute! One of those ducks wasn't a duck anymore. He had turned into a little boy. A little boy who looked exactly like Terry!

"IT'S ME—IT'S ME!" cried Terry.

And then the little boy rushed forward, up onto the land and jumped through the smoke ring toward Terry. Once outside the ring he turned into a duck again.

Terry blinked his eyes with disbelief.
"NO, IT'S *HIM! NOBODY!*"

Terry's old friend waddled up to him.
"Good to see you, Terry!" he said, giving the
boy a big bear hug—or rather, duck hug.
"Gee, you came all this way to find me?"

Terry nodded yes. "Un-huh. But when I
saw what you really were, I saw *me!*"

"Funny," said Nobody, "when I looked at
you from the other side of the smoke ring, I
saw *me!*"

Terry suddenly realized, "Then I must be
you—and you must be me!"

Nobody seemed a bit awed by the wonder
of it all. "What a great thing to happen to two
nice guys like us," he said.

47

Terry, still piecing together what it all meant, spoke slowly. "I guess that's why I could do all the stuff before. I mean, poems and pictures and music. It *was* him, as I thought. But it was also *me*! Are we the same person, Puff?"

"Well, that's hard to say," said Puff.

"Aw, Puff, you have to help explain—"

"Did I say I wouldn't?" smiled Puff. "When things are hard to say—you sing them!"

And that's exactly what they did. Oh, it was a joyous song that seemed to explain everything.

> *Imaginary friends—*
> *Are magic mirrors of your heart.*
> *They're partly you and partly me*
> *And partly they're apart!*
> *They can be balloons or blankets*
> *Rain or even rainbows,*
> *'Cause no one else can tell you*
> *How to think or how your brain goes!*
> *Believe in you, believe in me*
> *Believe in who you are.*
> *Believe in your own special self*
> *And follow your own star!*

Then, after all the singing and dancing, the three of them flopped down on the soft clover, exhausted.

"The same person. You and me. How about that?" said Terry, awed.

"And we always will be the same person. I promise!" said Nobody.

Terry's face lit up. "You mean you're coming back with me?"

Didn't say that," said the duck, troubled.

"See, the part of you that's *you*, belongs back home. And the part that's *me* belongs here. Your dad was right."

Terry sniffed back a tear. "Kind of sad."

"Yup," agreed Nobody.

"Ahem!" said Puff, a bit miffed at being left out in the cold. "If anyone cares, I have a solution. Nobody can come home with me."

"With you?" said Terry. "Is Honah Lee part of the Fantaverse?"

Puff smiled. "No farther away than the flight of a kite."

"Gee," said Terry, realizing, "if Nobody was with you, it'd be like I was with you. We'd all be together." He rushed over to Nobody. "Will you go with Puff?" he asked the duck.

"Sure," said Nobody, winking at the dragon, "I thought he'd never ask me."

Terry and Nobody laughed. Puff was about to reply, when suddenly he remembered something. He reached into his left pocket and took out his old alarm clock, which he kept as lesser folk kept gold watches, on a chain.

"Dear me, it's later than I think again," said Puff. "We'd best be on our way."

Terry and Nobody stopped laughing

suddenly, for both realized that the time for parting had come. They faced each other awkwardly.

"Aw, Nobody, you're the best friend a guy could ever have."

"You're tops too," said the duck. "If I had a middle name, *Terry* would be it!"

Then the little boy and the silly duck felt something so big and beautiful, so warm and wonderful, so strong and real that words, pictures and even music could not express it. They rushed to each other and embraced fondly, one and the same, forever.

Puff watched, off to the side, smiled, then reached into his right pocket. He brought out a huge kite. He let it go up, holding only the string. "There's an east wind to Honah Lee," he said gently. "Mustn't lose it."

The part of Terry which was Nobody pulled himself away and grabbed onto the kite string, just below Puff. Then they sailed off into the lovely sky.

The part of Terry that was Terry stayed behind, watching them go off, higher and higher. Next to him was a lilac bush. He climbed up into it, as if to stay as close as possible to his friends.

But wait a minute!

There were no lilac bushes by the duckpond.

These were the lilac bushes in Terry's own backyard!

Terry looked about. It wasn't daytime anymore. Suddenly it was night again. Then he heard his mother's voice cry out, "TERRY!"

He heard his father say, "He's in the lilacs! The bush must have broken his fall!"

Terry realized that he was in the lilac bush that grew right beneath his bedroom window. The loose bedsheet rope dangled above him.

"Mom? Dad?" he called.

His parents rushed to him. His father lifted him down, and both embraced him soundly.

"Darling, are you hurt?" asked his mother.

"No," said Terry, feeling all his bones and finding them solid. "But the rope broke. And I fell. And then..."

"Why were you climbing out of the window, son?" asked his father.

"To find Nobody. And I found him! And do you know where he was? Inside of me all the time. And that's where he always *will* be.

And do you know what else?"

"What?" said his mother.

"I've got to practice my piano!" he roared, dashing off. "My own song!" he added, as he ran into the house.

Terry's mother and father hadn't the slightest idea what had come over their very remarkable young son. And they realized they probably never would fully understand what went on inside him. Best to give him all the love they could and, like the rest of the world, enjoy how magnificently special he was.

And if the whole wide world was to be Terry's audience, then a very special duck and an *extremely* special dragon would certainly be seated in the very first row.

Songs

Never Was a Feather

Words and music by Peter Yarrow

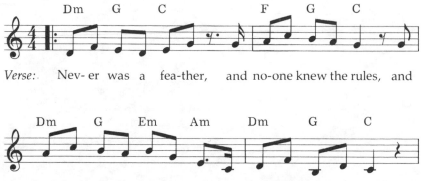

Verse: Nev-er was a fea-ther, and no-one knew the rules, and

that's how all the cher-ries went to squish in squish-y pools.

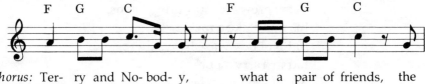

Chorus: Ter- ry and No- bod- y,   what a pair of friends, the

lim- its   were   the   skies   a- bove   and

where the rain-bows end.   ma-gic drag-ons know.

Verse 2: Spoons turned into lollipops,
then forests red and blue.
Terry's wish for a special friend
had finally come true.

Chorus 2: They laughed and played the whole year long,
the months, they just flew past.
And now young Terry, he was six,
and school came at last.

Verse 3: Terry outgrew his trousers,
but not his special friend.
Together they did everything
from morning to day's end.

Chorus 3: Terry grew like sprouting beans,
his mind like a rocket,
But Nobody was always there,
hid in Terry's pocket.

Verse 4: Never ain't forever
when teacher makes the rules,
and squishy cherries just don't float,
at least in Terry's school.

Verse 5: Terry was so hurt and sad,
so his talent he just hid it.
When someone said, "Did you do that?"
he said, "Nobody did it!"

Chorus 5: Soon he believed that all his talent
came from his dear friend.
Sometimes we talk ourselves into
what starts out as pretend.

Chorus 6: It's sad, I know, it once was told
in some old dragon song,
when children learn that pretend friends
can't stay the whole life long.

Verse 6: Imagined ducks are wonderful,
but then it's time to grow.
It's so hard to say good-bye,
as we magic dragons know.

Imaginary Friends

Words and music by Peter Yarrow

(1) I- ma- gin- a- ry friends are ma- gic

mir- rors of your heart. They're part- ly you and part- ly me, and

part- ly they're a- part.   They can be bal- loons or blan- kets,

rain, or e- ven rain-bows 'cause no-one else can tell you how to

think or where your brain goes.   Be-

lieve in you, be- lieve in me, be- lieve in who you are.   Be-

lieve in your own spe-cial self,   and fol-low your own star. Be-

lieve in you, be-lieve in me, be- lieve in who you are.   Be-

lieve in your own spe-cial self,   and   fol-low your own star.

D. S. al ⊕   ⊕   (Am)   D

I-   lieve in your own spe-cial self,   and

fol- low   your own   star.

(2) Imaginary friends are just as real as sleepy dreams.
Dragons! Castles! Pirates! Ducks!
Who knows what all that means.
And when you wake up you remember parts to tell your friends,
so that's the way to make a dream that never, never ends.
Believe in you, believe in me, believe in who you are.
Believe in your own special self, and follow your own star.

(3) Imaginary friends are just like hopes that might come true.
One part smiles, one part tears, but all parts, part of you.
The specialness that each one has unique in all creation
is found, I do believe my friends, in your imagination.
Believe in you, believe in me, believe in who you are.
Believe in your own special self, and follow your own star.